THE TALE OF

MR JEREMY FISHER

BEATRIX POTTER

OCTOPUS BOOKS INC

O NCE upon a time there was a frog called Mr Jeremy Fisher; he lived in a little damp house amongst the butter-cups at the edge of a pond.

The water was all slippy-sloppy in the larder and in the back passage.

But Mr Jeremy liked getting his feet wet; nobody ever scolded him, and he never caught a cold!

He was quite pleased when he looked out and saw large drops of rain, splashing in the pond —

'I will get some worms and go fishing and catch a dish of minnows for my dinner,' said Mr Jeremy Fisher.

'If I catch more than five fish, I will invite my friends Mr Alderman Ptolemy Tortoise and Sir Isaac Newton. The Alderman, however, eats salad.'

Mr Jeremy put on a macintosh, and a pair of shiny galoshes; he took his rod and basket, and set off with enormous hops to the place where he kept his boat.

The boat was round and green, and very like the other lily-leaves. It was tied to a water-plant in the middle of the pond.

Mr Jeremy took a reed pole, and pushed the boat out into open water. 'I know a good place for minnows,' said Mr Jeremy Fisher.

Mr Jeremy stuck his pole into the mud and fastened his boat to it.

Then he settled himself cross-legged and arranged his fishing tackle. He had the dearest little red float. His rod was a tough stalk of grass, his line was a fine long white horse-hair, and he tied a little wriggling worm at the end.

The rain trickled down his back, and for nearly an hour he stared at the float.

'This is getting tiresome, I think I should like some lunch,' said Mr Jeremy Fisher.

He punted back again amongst the water-plants, and took some lunch out of his basket.

'I will eat a butterfly sandwich, and wait till the shower is over,' said Mr Jeremy Fisher.

A great big water-beetle came up underneath the lily leaf and tweaked the toe of one of his galoshes.

Mr Jeremy crossed his legs up shorter, out of reach, and went on eating his sandwich.

Once or twice something moved about with a rustle and a splash amongst the rushes at the side of the pond.

'I trust that is not a rat,' said Mr Jeremy Fisher; 'I think I had better get away from here.'

Mr Jeremy shoved the boat out again a little way, and dropped in the bait. There was a bite almost directly; the float gave a tremendous bobbit!

'A minnow! a minnow! I have him by the nose!' cried Mr Jeremy Fisher, jerking up his rod.

But what a horrible surprise! Instead of a smooth fat minnow, Mr Jeremy landed little Jack Sharp the stickleback, covered with spines!

The stickleback floundered about the boat, pricking and snapping until he was quite out of breath. Then he jumped back into the water.

And a shoal of other little fishes
put their heads out, and laughed
at Mr Jeremy Fisher.

And while Mr Jeremy sat disconsolately on the edge of his boat — sucking his sore fingers and peering down into the water — a *much* worse thing happened; a really *frightful* thing it would have been, if Mr Jeremy had not been wearing a macintosh!

A great big enormous trout came up — ker-pflop-p-p-p! with a splash — and it seized Mr Jeremy with a snap, 'Ow! Ow! Ow!' — and then it turned and dived down to the bottom of the pond!

But the trout was so displeased
with the taste of the macintosh,
that in less than half a minute it
spat him out again; and the only
thing it swallowed was Mr
Jeremy's galoshes.

Mr Jeremy bounced up to the surface of the water, like a cork and the bubbles out of a soda water bottle; and he swam with all his might to the edge of the pond.

He scrambled out on the first bank he came to, and he hopped home across the meadow with his macintosh all in tatters.

'What a mercy that was not a pike!' said Mr Jeremy Fisher. 'I have lost my rod and basket; but it does not much matter, for I am sure I should never have dared to go fishing again!'

He put some sticking plaster on his fingers, and his friends both came to dinner. He could not offer them fish, but he had something else in his larder.

Sir Isaac Newton wore his black and gold waistcoat.

And Mr Alderman Ptolemy Tortoise brought a salad with him in a string bag.

And instead of a nice dish of minnows — they had a roasted grasshopper with lady-bird sauce; which frogs consider a beautiful treat; but I think it must have been nasty!

THE END

This edition © 1986 Octopus Books Inc
ISBN: 1-55580-004-1
Printed in the United States of America